Merry Ever After

The Story of Two Medieval Weddings

Written and illustrated by

Joe Lasker

Puffin Books

For David

First published by The Viking Press 1976
Published in Puffin Books 1978
Reprinted 1986

Library of Congress Cataloging in Publication Data
Lasker, Joe.   Merry ever after.
Summary: Contrasts the way children of different social
classes were betrothed and married during the Middle Ages.
1. Marriage customs and rites, Medieval—Juvenile
literature. [1. Civilization, Medieval. 2. Marriage
customs and rites, Medieval] I. Title.
[GT2680.L37 1978]   392'.5'094   78-3730
ISBN 0 14 050.280 7

Manufactured in the U.S.A. by
Lake Book/Cuneo, Inc., Melrose Park, IL

he days of knights and castles were long ago, yet we still find them interesting. Perhaps that is because we know that even though the parents and children of medieval Europe wore different clothing, ate odd foods (mostly with their fingers), and lived in strange kinds of houses, they were still like us. We can see something of ourselves in these distant people because many of our customs and beliefs started in olden times — wedding customs, for example. Old writings and beautiful drawings and paintings tell us this. All the pictures in this book of people and animals, castles and cottages, are based on paintings or pictures that were drawn by artists who lived a long time ago. The children and the parents in this story are made up, but the things they did and the way they lived are true, in general, for the Middle Ages.

This story of a noble wedding and a peasant wedding is like an old mirror, cracked and curved, but still one in which we can see ourselves reflected.

From these artists came inspiration and visual information; all were active in the fifteenth century (except Bruegel, who worked in the sixteenth century): Fouquet, The Limbourg Brothers, Pisanello, Carpaccio, Uccello, Mantegna, Bosch, Van der Weyden, Dürer, Bruegel, the Master of King René, the Master of Mary of Burgundy, the Master of Catherine of Cleves, the Master of the Hausbuch, the craftsmen of the Flemish and French tapestry workshops, and anonymous illuminators and miniaturists.

J.L.

Anne was only ten years old when her father told her she would marry Gilbert, who was eleven. Anne had never met Gilbert. She would not meet him until her wedding day, when she would be fifteen. Anne was not upset to find out she was betrothed to Gilbert. In fifteenth-century Europe it was the custom for parents to arrange a marriage for their children.

Anne's father was a rich merchant. His ships traded in foreign ports. Someday my daughter will need a husband, he had thought. And so he and Gilbert's father had met.

Gilbert's father, a noble lord, said proudly, "I own wide fields, thick forests, and fish-filled waters. I also own the people who live on my land. My serfs work for me, and I allow them to build their houses and villages on my land. Someday my son will own all this. He will need a wife."

"Your serfs will need seed and tools and fishing nets to harvest your lands and waters," Anne's father had replied.

"But the battles I have fought were costly," sighed Gilbert's father. "My peasants were soldiers too long. While they were away fighting in strange lands, the crops withered and died. There was no one to repair the castle or shoe the horses. Now that there is peace I need help in rebuilding my land and property."

Anne's father knew that this marriage would enable him to share in the lord's property and noble name. "I was born a commoner," he said, "but my family can become noble through marriage. If your son and my daughter marry, it would be a simple favor for my banks and my ships to supply all your needs. Good times would come to both our families."

Gilbert's father nodded. "Then let us agree: the betrothal of my son and your daughter will bring our families together, and we will help each other." The merchant and the lord shook hands and embraced. They did not ask Anne and Gilbert how they felt about their betrothal.

he years passed. Gilbert grew up in his father's castle. Most of the time his father was away with his soldiers and knights, fighting wars. There were few men left in the castle, and Gilbert was lonely. He played with his sisters, who teased him because he was the youngest. His mother fussed over him when she wasn't busy managing the castle and its lands during her husband's absence.

Gilbert's father, home for a while between wars, became concerned for his son. "If you continue to stay here with your mother and sisters, you will grow soft. I want you to live in your uncle's castle and serve with his knights."

Gilbert left for his uncle's castle to prepare for noble manhood. He quickly found that he enjoyed spending time with his uncle's knights, learning the skills of war, hunting, and horsemanship. In the castle he studied reading, writing, and manners. The years went by, and soon Gilbert was sixteen.

During those same years, Anne lived in her father's manor house, leaving only to attend church, accompanied by her relatives and her nurse.

At home, Anne learned how to cook. She was taught to weave and to play music. And, since the mistress of a household would also have to be its doctor, she learned about sicknesses and how to cure them by making medicines from plants and herbs.

The betrothal now pleased Anne. When she was married she could leave her parents' house and her parents' watchful eyes and have her own home. She knew that if she did not marry, she would have to live in a convent as a nun, and she didn't want to do that. Her nurse had told her, "After marriage, a girl enjoys life. When you manage a household you will make your own decisions."

ecause everything depended so much on the activities of the wealthy lord and merchant, the friendship of the two families and the approaching wedding brought good times to the people. Flocks grazed in pastures that had once been overgrown with weeds. Plowmen cheerfully drove their oxen in fields that had not been planted for years.

Masons and carpenters repaired the castles and cottages.

Tailors worked long hours, cutting and sewing fine clothing for the nobility to wear to the wedding.

Weavers wove picture stories on big tapestry rugs that were to hang on the walls for decoration and warmth. They showed the lord as a brave warrior in battle and the merchant as a wealthy man with many great ships.

Cabinet makers carved the intertwined initials of the two families into rich dark wood.

On the day of the wedding everyone celebrated. A merry carnival spirit filled the crowded town square. Jugglers, acrobats, minstrels, and dancing bears performed to happy crowds under colorful banners.

utside the merchant's house beggars gathered, waiting. After the feast all the leftover food would be given to them. The merchant could well be generous since there was little that could be done to preserve the food or prevent it from spoiling.

Wardens unlocked their dungeons and freed the prisoners.
Tenants and landlords set aside their arguments.
The wedding guests pressed eagerly into the merchant's house, looking forward to the good food, dancing, and entertainment.

They passed through the great hall, where musicians played from a balcony. From there they crowded into the chapel and waited.

Gilbert was nervous. It's all so strange, he thought. Yesterday I was a boy, hunting with my uncle's rough knights. Now I'm sixteen, wearing splendid robes, about to be married. I am going to marry a girl I have never seen or talked to.

Anne too was nervous. In the side room where she waited, she thought, Here in my father's house, I begin a strange new life. Suddenly I am a grownup, changed from girl to woman by a wedding ring. My new master's name is Gilbert. It might as well be Albert or Humbert, for all I know of him! I hope he will be gentle and kind so that I may like him.

The marriage ceremony began. As Anne and Gilbert stopped being frightened, they could relax and study each other. Each saw a friendly shy face. At last the bridal cup was passed to Anne and then Gilbert; they sipped the spiced wine and smiled. Their pleased parents also smiled. The archbishop smiled too as he spoke the blessing. All the guests smiled. A warm and friendly feeling spread through the chapel.

On the very same day, in one of the lord's distant villages, another marriage was taking place. But riches and noble titles were not part of Martha and Simon's betrothal.

Their marriage agreement had been simpler. Martha's father, who was a blacksmith, had told the other serfs that he was ready to give his daughter in marriage.

imon's father, a plowman, had been interested: "Your Martha is fourteen, old enough to take a husband," he had said. Martha stood behind her father but said nothing.

"Your Simon is sixteen; he can take a wife," the blacksmith had replied. Simon too was silent.

"Martha will need a dowry of gifts to get a husband," the plowman said.

"Her dowry will be a goose, a goat, and land for a cottage," answered Martha's father.

"The dowry should include a strip of farmland," Simon's father added hopefully.

"The lord charges a fee when a daughter marries," grumbled the blacksmith. "He also charges when someone takes over new land. I don't have enough money to buy farmland for Simon and also pay the fees."

Simon's father thought it over; then he said, "The old widow who lives alone at the village edge will be selling her land one day. Promise to buy it then for Simon, and our children will be betrothed." The two men smiled and shook hands. They did not ask Martha and Simon how they felt about their betrothal.

Martha and Simon had always known each other and did not question their fathers' choice. Since childhood they had worked alongside their parents. Simon was also a plowman. The children had never been away from their small village, and like everyone else in it, they could neither read nor write. Martha's brothers had learned from their father how to be blacksmiths, while

Martha had learned from her mother to raise chickens, cows, and other animals. Martha had cared for her younger brothers and sisters from the time they were born. Both Martha and Simon could expect their future to be much the same as their past; they would always work hard on the lord's land, and so would their children.

One day, Simon would have to leave his wife and village to follow his lord into war.

The peasants had never heard stories of love and romance;

while in the castle, ''romance'' was a new fashion, spread by minstrels who traveled from castle to castle, entertaining their noble listeners with love stories and poems set to music.

One Sunday, Martha's bridesmaid and Simon's groomsman drove a hay wagon around the village, collecting gifts for the couple. "Simon is taking Martha to wife!" they called. In response, the villagers gave stools, a wooden tub, a brush, a pail, a pitchfork, some tools, some ladles, wooden cups and bowls, and a crib.

The wagon carried the gifts to the cottage of Simon's parents, where the couple would first live. In cottage as in castle, life was crowded. Small children slept in their parents' bed; older children slept on the floor, along with the dogs, pigs, and chickens. Privacy, or the idea that each person needed a place to himself in a house, was unknown.

On the wedding day, a bagpiper played a cheerful tune and led the wedding procession. Martha, with two small boys at her side, carried ears of wheat in her arms. It meant she wished her family would never go hungry. Behind followed her mother, Simon's mother, and the bridesmaid; then came the women and girls of the village, carrying trays of small bridal cakes.

Martha's and Simon's thoughts were on their new life. She said to herself, "I will soon have my own family and my own house, my own garden and my own animals. That will be better than sharing with my parents and brothers." Simon thought, We will build a warm cottage and have many children. The more children we have, the more help we will have. The more help we have, the more land and animals we can have. The more land and animals we have, the better off we will be.

The squealing bagpipes mixed with the clanging bells as the procession reached the church, where a churchman and the lord's steward waited at the door. The steward was the lord's cousin and looked after his lands. Because he was related to the lord, he was an important man, and his presence made the wedding special. Martha and Simon held hands as the churchman blessed their marriage. Instead of a gold ring, Simon gave Martha half a broken coin, keeping the other half for himself. Now they were two halves of a whole.

The newlyweds left the church and the young women of the village showered them with seeds and grains of wheat, meant to wish them many children. At the tables, Martha and Simon, the guests of honor, sat on the only chairs with backs.

The feasting began. There were poultry and game, pork, fish, and mutton, prepared over crackling fires and served with sauces and puddings. There were huge cheeses and hot soups, beef stews and meat pies. The loaves of bread were dark and coarse-grained—only the lord could afford soft, white bread. For dessert there were fruit fritters and stewed fruit, fruit tarts and fruit pancakes. Fruit and honey, cooked to a solid, were cut into candy-like strips and served cold. Wine, beer, ale, and cider flowed freely from big wooden barrels. Tea and coffee were not yet known, and plain water, which might not be pure, was thought unsafe to drink.

Even though the two weddings were different in many ways, the behavior of the guests was much the same. At the tables, two people shared the same dish and cup. They ate with their fingers and lifted bowls to their mouths. The only eating tool was the

knife or dagger that men and some women carried with them and used for other things as well. Forks were not yet in use; only a few rich people knew of spoons. It was proper to wipe off sticky fingers on bread.

Then the waiting bagpiper struck up a happy tune; a rollicking
peasant dance began. The dancers went round and round, faster
and faster, bumping each other in the crowded circle of tables
and benches borrowed from the cottages.

Both celebrations had shouting, dancing, quarrels, and fighting. Dogs joined in, battling for bones and scraps of food tossed away by the diners.

The wedding of Anne and Gilbert went on for two weeks, as was fitting for a rich bride and groom.

The merrymaking at the wedding of Martha and Simon lasted
for two days. The peasants drank and grew wild. This was their
escape from hard work. The piper played, the dancers danced.
Then, worn out, they dropped one by one, sleeping where they
fell.

The wedding of Martha and Simon was over.
The wedding of Anne and Gilbert was over.
Martha and Simon in their cottage, like Anne and Gilbert in their castle, lived together ever after.

Some Other Picture Puffins

The Amazing Bone   *William Steig*
Amos and Boris   *William Steig*
Anansi the Spider   *Gerald McDermott*
Arrow to the Sun   *Gerald McDermott*

392.5
LAS

a L3R 1B4

Merry Ever After

Written and illustrated by

Joe Lasker